yoko tsuno
electronics engineer

by Roger Leloup

THE ARCHANGELS OF VINEA

9th CINEBOOK
The 9th Art Publisher

Original title: Yoko Tsuno – Les archanges de Vinéa
Original edition: © Dupuis, 1983 by Roger Leloup
www.dupuis.com

English translation: © 2019 Cinebook Ltd
Translator: Jerome Saincantin
Editor: Erica Olson Jeffrey
Lettering and text layout: Design Amorandi
Printed in Spain by EGEDSA
This edition first published in Great Britain in 2019 by
Cinebook Ltd
56 Beech Avenue
Canterbury, Kent
CT4 7TA
www.cinebook.com
A CIP catalogue record for this book
is available from the British Library
ISBN 978-1-84918-438-0

9th CINEBOOK
The 9th Art Publisher

TWO MILLION LIGHT YEARS AWAY FROM EARTH, IN THE TRIANGULUM GALAXY, VINEA ALWAYS KEEPS THE SAME SIDE TO HER TWIN SUNS AS SHE ORBITS THEM ... THAT SIDE IS SCORCHED BY THE HEAT — WHILE THE OTHER IS ENCASED IN DARKNESS AND ICE ...

BETWEEN THOSE TWO HELLISH LANDSCAPES, THE VINEANS, USING CLIMATIC BARRIERS, HAVE CREATED A HABITABLE TEMPERATE ZONE ...

THERE, WATER AND LAND COMPETE FOR THE AVAILABLE SPACE IN SOMETIMES SURREAL LANDSCAPES ...

SURPRISING, ISN'T IT, YOKO?

IT IS, KHANY! SO MANY ISLANDS ... INHABITED?

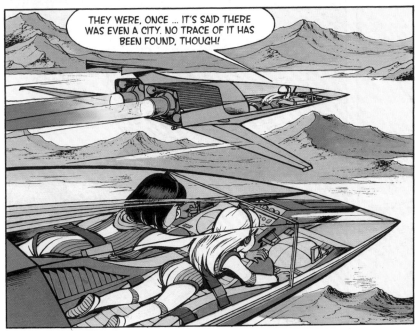

THEY WERE, ONCE ... IT'S SAID THERE WAS EVEN A CITY. NO TRACE OF IT HAS BEEN FOUND, THOUGH!

A CITY! ... WITH CHILDREN?

OF COURSE, POKY! THERE CAN'T BE A CITY WITHOUT CHILDREN.

THAT ONE WAS CERTAINLY NOT SHORT ON THEM. ALMOST AS IF IT HAD BEEN BUILT FOR THEM!

I DON'T FOLLOW ... YOU DOUBT THAT CITY'S VERY EXISTENCE YET CAN SPECIFY THE NATURE OF ITS INHABITANTS?!

THEY ARE WHAT JUSTIFIES THE POSSIBILITY THAT THE CITY WAS REAL ...

THE ENTIRE POPULATION OF VINEA, PAST AND PRESENT, IS MAGNETICALLY RECORDED AND KEPT TRACK OF FROM BIRTH TO DEATH ... FOR HALF A MILLION CHILDREN, THOUGH, ALL RECORDS STOP ON THE DAY THEY LEFT FOR A CITY THAT COULD NEVER BE LOCATED ... THAT WAS ABOUT TWO THOUSAND OF YOUR YEARS AGO.

TWO THOUSAND! THEY'RE ALL GONE, NOW.

GONE? ...

EXCEPT ONE! ...
WHOM I FOUND!

IT'S HIM I'M TAKING YOU TO SEE. BEGINNING DESCENT NOW.

THE TWO AIRCRAFT SHED ALTITUDE QUICKLY ...

WE'RE HERE! LET'S LAND.

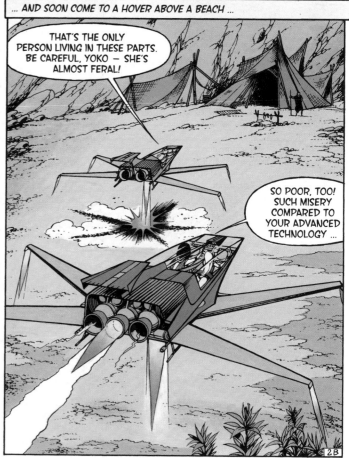

... AND SOON COME TO A HOVER ABOVE A BEACH ...

THAT'S THE ONLY PERSON LIVING IN THESE PARTS. BE CAREFUL, YOKO — SHE'S ALMOST FERAL!

SO POOR, TOO! SUCH MISERY COMPARED TO YOUR ADVANCED TECHNOLOGY ...

4

YOU CAME BACK WITH THAT STRANGER TO TAKE THE CHILD FROM ME!

YOU'RE WRONG.

MY FRIEND IS FROM ANOTHER WORLD. I TOLD HER HOW BEAUTIFUL YOUR CHILD IS, AND SHE WOULD LIKE TO SEE HIM ...

AND THIS ONE? ...

MY SISTER. SHE CAME A LONG WAY TO SEE YOUR 'SON' ...

FEAR NOT, CHILD. TEARS MAY HAVE FURROWED MY FACE, BUT MY HEART HAS REMAINED LIKE YOURS!

POKY IS TERRIFIED ... DON'T LEAVE HER ALONE WITH THIS POOR, MAD WOMAN. I'LL JOIN YOU IN A MINUTE!

I'M GOING TO SHOW YOU MY CHILD ... BUT YOU MUST BE QUIET ...

... FOR HE SLEEPS, AND NO ONE IS ALLOWED TO AWAKEN HIM ...

OH! THAT CHILD IS IN A MAGNETIC LETHARGY POD ...

HERE IS THE SON THE GOD GAVE ME!

WE'RE ABOUT TO FIND OUT WHEN THAT CHILD WAS PUT TO SLEEP ...

THE METAL OF THE POD APPEARS CORRODED IN PLACES ...

THAT'S BECAUSE IT SPENT A LONG TIME IN THE WATER!

THE WATER?!!

OH? STRANGE! THERE'S A POWERFUL MAGNETIC FIELD INTERFERING WITH THE ANALYSER ... AND IT'S NOT COMING FROM THE POD!

5

SUDDENLY ...

WOOOOOOOOOO'...

LISTEN!

THAT'S OUTSIDE!

THE WOMEN RUSH OUT OF THE TENT ...

THERE! ON THE HORIZON – IT LOOKS LIKE THE SEA IS BOILING!

AN ANIMAL? ... NO – IT WOULD BE COLOSSAL!

THAT'S THE GOD CALLING NEW VICTIMS!

WHOOOOOOOOOOO'....

I'LL GO AND TAKE A CLOSER LOOK. STAY HERE WITH POKY!

DON'T GO!

SHE WON'T COME BACK! NONE OF THOSE WHO SEE THE GOD EVER COME BACK!

WHEEEEEE

BOTH OF MY SONS WENT. THEY WANTED TO KNOW TOO ... THE GOD TOOK THEM FROM ME AND IN RETURN, PUNISHED ME WITH THIS CHILD TRAPPED IN ETERNAL SLUMBER ...

POOR WOMAN ... OH, KHANY'S CALLING!

YOKO?!

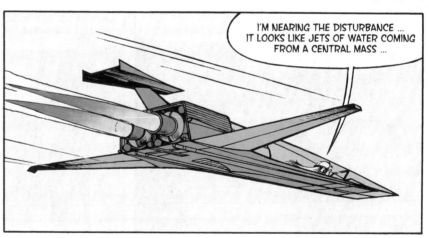

I'M NEARING THE DISTURBANCE ... IT LOOKS LIKE JETS OF WATER COMING FROM A CENTRAL MASS ...

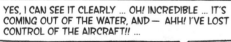

YES, I CAN SEE IT CLEARLY ... OH! INCREDIBLE ... IT'S COMING OUT OF THE WATER, AND — AHH! I'VE LOST CONTROL OF THE AIRCRAFT!! ...

YOKO ... WARN ... OTHERS ... DON'T ... CRSHH ... TWEEEEP ...

KHANY'S IN TROUBLE ... POKY, YOU STAY HERE. I—

I'M COMING WITH YOU!

NO!

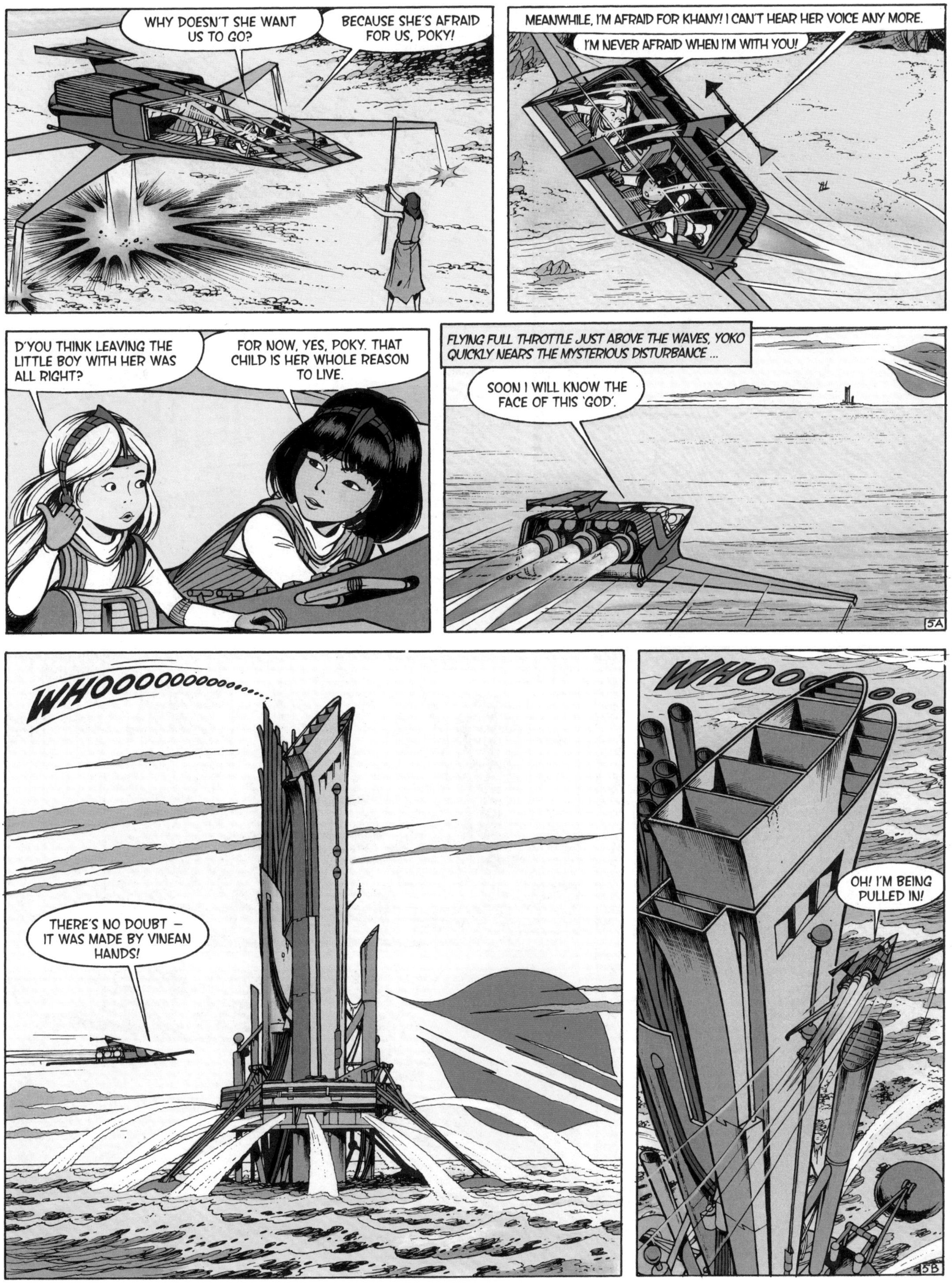
WHY DOESN'T SHE WANT US TO GO?
BECAUSE SHE'S AFRAID FOR US, POKY!
MEANWHILE, I'M AFRAID FOR KHANY! I CAN'T HEAR HER VOICE ANY MORE.
I'M NEVER AFRAID WHEN I'M WITH YOU!
D'YOU THINK LEAVING THE LITTLE BOY WITH HER WAS ALL RIGHT?
FOR NOW, YES, POKY. THAT CHILD IS HER WHOLE REASON TO LIVE.
FLYING FULL THROTTLE JUST ABOVE THE WAVES, YOKO QUICKLY NEARS THE MYSTERIOUS DISTURBANCE ...
SOON I WILL KNOW THE FACE OF THIS 'GOD'.
5A
WHOOOOOOOOOOOOOOOO....
THERE'S NO DOUBT – IT WAS MADE BY VINEAN HANDS!
WHOOOOOOO
OH! I'M BEING PULLED IN!
5B

BANKING HARD, YOKO WRESTS THE AIRCRAFT AWAY FROM THE STACK ...

WHOA! I NEARLY GOT SUCKED IN!! THAT THING TAKES IN TONS OF AIR ...

... AND SPITS OUT WATER VAPOUR ... THERE! KHANY'S AIRCRAFT!

D'YOU SEE KHANY? ...

NO. THE COCKPIT IS OPENED BUT EMPTY. LET'S LAND!

SHE APPEARS TO HAVE MADE A NORMAL LANDING, BUT HER VANISHING ISN'T NORMAL AT ALL!

THIS SUDDEN SILENCE, NOW!! IT'S LIKE ...

POKY, STAY INSIDE!

YES! THIS GIANT MACHINE HAS STOPPED ... AND IS SINKING!

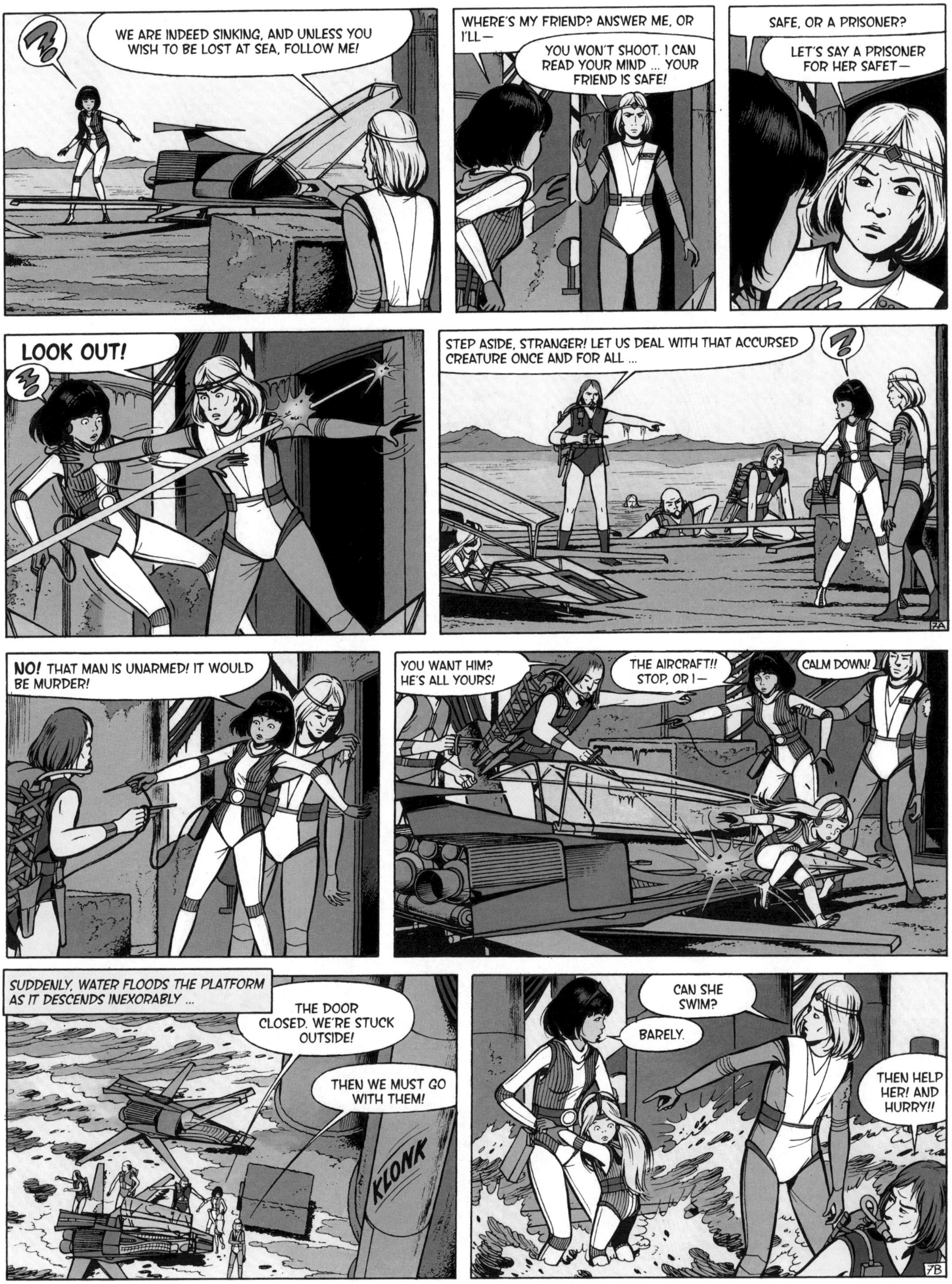
WE ARE INDEED SINKING, AND UNLESS YOU WISH TO BE LOST AT SEA, FOLLOW ME!
WHERE'S MY FRIEND? ANSWER ME, OR I'LL—
YOU WON'T SHOOT. I CAN READ YOUR MIND ... YOUR FRIEND IS SAFE!
SAFE, OR A PRISONER?
LET'S SAY A PRISONER FOR HER SAFET—
LOOK OUT!
STEP ASIDE, STRANGER! LET US DEAL WITH THAT ACCURSED CREATURE ONCE AND FOR ALL ...
7A
NO! THAT MAN IS UNARMED! IT WOULD BE MURDER!
YOU WANT HIM? HE'S ALL YOURS!
THE AIRCRAFT!! STOP, OR I—
CALM DOWN!
SUDDENLY, WATER FLOODS THE PLATFORM AS IT DESCENDS INEXORABLY ...
THE DOOR CLOSED. WE'RE STUCK OUTSIDE!
THEN WE MUST GO WITH THEM!
KLONK
CAN SHE SWIM?
BARELY.
THEN HELP HER! AND HURRY!!
7B

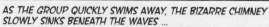

AS THE GROUP QUICKLY SWIMS AWAY, THE BIZARRE CHIMNEY SLOWLY SINKS BENEATH THE WAVES ...

RAFTS?! THAT SEEMS A LITTLE CRUDE ...

READY TWO LINES!

CAN THE CHILD BREATHE WITH THIS?

LET'S TRY.

WHATEVER YOU DO, DON'T TAKE OUT THE LITTLE BALLS THAT BLOCK YOUR NOSE! BREATHE IN AND OUT THROUGH THE HOSE ... AND TO 'SPEAK', USE YOUR THOUGHT TRANSMITTER. ALL RIGHT?

MMM ... ARE YOU TAKING A HOSE TOO?

OF COURSE, LIKE EVERYONE ELSE. HERE.

GREAT ... WE'VE WASTED ENOUGH TIME. LET'S DIVE — KEEP UP!

INCREDIBLE! ... THESE THINGS ARE MASSIVE YET COMPLETELY DOCILE ...

WE'RE DRAGGING THE RAFT ALONG ... WHY DID THEY GIVE US DIFFERENT BREATHING GEAR THAN THEIR OWN ...

... BUT DIDN'T GIVE ANY TO THE MAN I PROTECTED AS IF HE WERE MY OWN BROTHER?

9A

STRANGE! THE MORE I LOOK AT HIM, THE MORE I'M CONVINCED HE'S NOT BREATHING ... IS HE ADAPTED TO UNDERWATER LIFE? ...

THE RUINS OF A CITY!

... AND EVEN STRANGER, IT'S AS IF SOMETHING INSIDE ME WERE PUSHING ME TO FOLLOW HIM ... TRUST HIM ...

MMMM ... LOOK!

9B

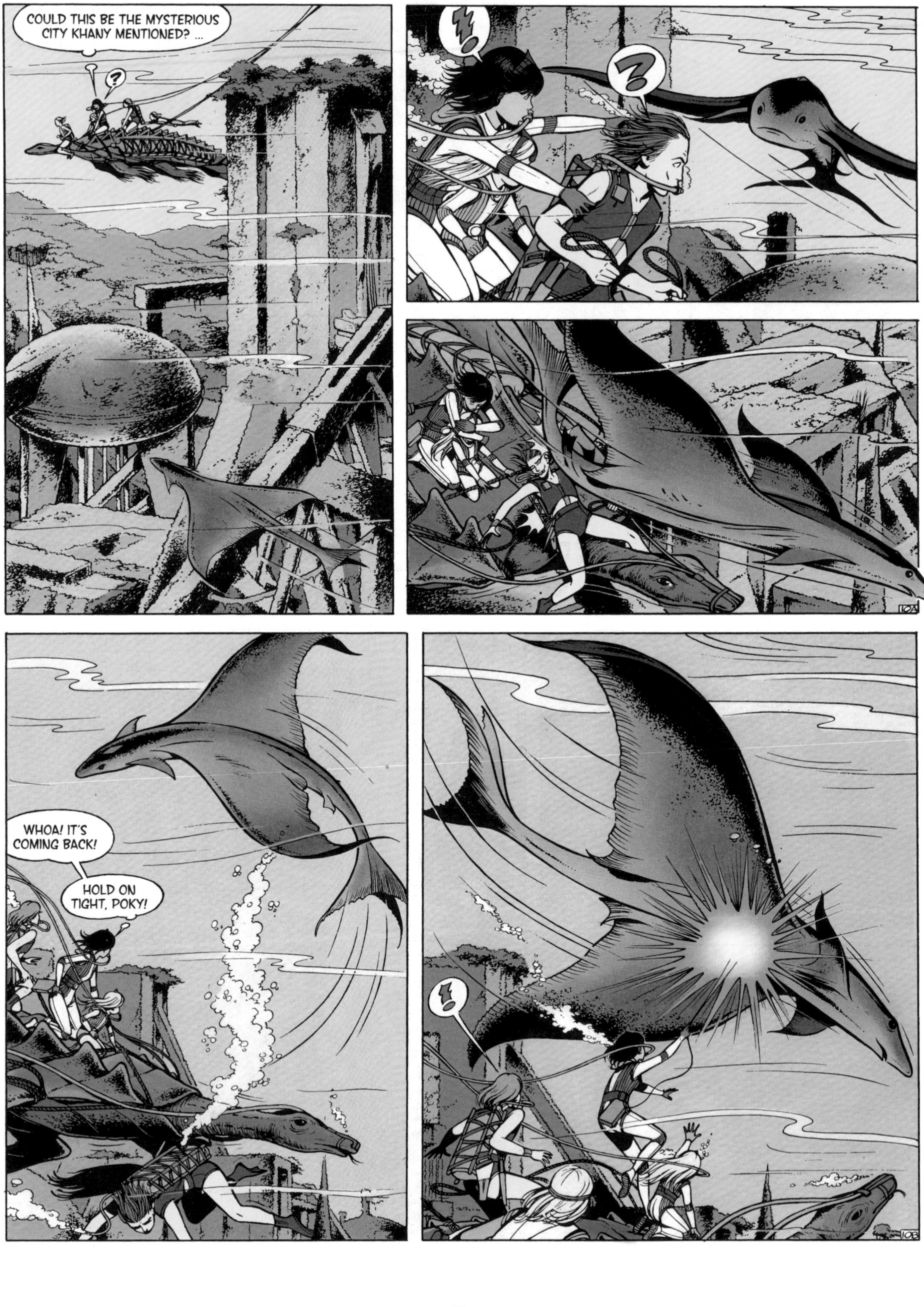
COULD THIS BE THE MYSTERIOUS CITY KHANY MENTIONED? ...
?
!
?
WHOA! IT'S COMING BACK!
HOLD ON TIGHT, POKY!
!

AS THE BEAST CONVULSES ONE LAST TIME ...

HIS BACKPACK IS DAMAGED!

WAIT!

I'LL LEND HIM MY HOSE ...

NO!

YOUR AIR WOULD BURN HIS LUNGS! LET HIS COMPANION TAKE CARE OF HIM.

MMPFF ...

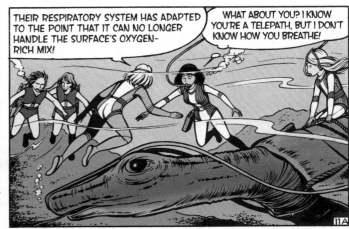

THEIR RESPIRATORY SYSTEM HAS ADAPTED TO THE POINT THAT IT CAN NO LONGER HANDLE THE SURFACE'S OXYGEN-RICH MIX!

WHAT ABOUT YOU? I KNOW YOU'RE A TELEPATH, BUT I DON'T KNOW HOW YOU BREATHE!

YOU WILL KNOW SOON, BUT FOR NOW WE MUST LEAVE, QUICKLY ... THIS MAY NOT HAVE BEEN THE STYR'S DOING ...

THE GROUP RESUMES ITS PROGRESS, AND SOON ...

THIS IS THE PART OF THE CITY WHERE THESE PEOPLE LIVE.

OH? AND ... THE OTHERS?

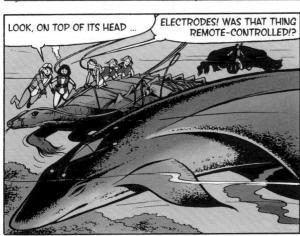

LOOK, ON TOP OF ITS HEAD ...

ELECTRODES! WAS THAT THING REMOTE-CONTROLLED!?

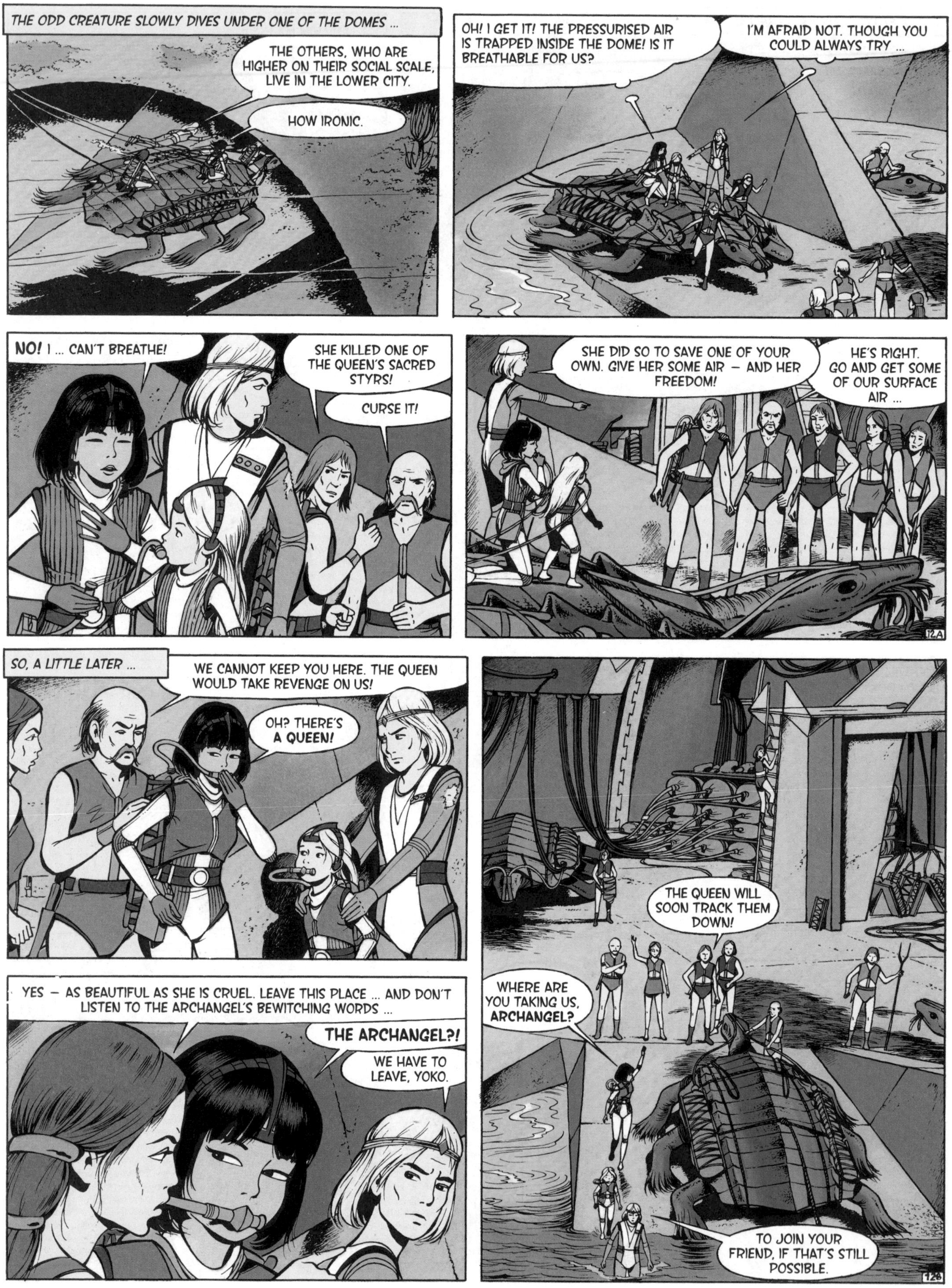
THE ODD CREATURE SLOWLY DIVES UNDER ONE OF THE DOMES ...
THE OTHERS, WHO ARE HIGHER ON THEIR SOCIAL SCALE, LIVE IN THE LOWER CITY.
HOW IRONIC.
OH! I GET IT! THE PRESSURISED AIR IS TRAPPED INSIDE THE DOME! IS IT BREATHABLE FOR US?
I'M AFRAID NOT. THOUGH YOU COULD ALWAYS TRY ...
NO! I ... CAN'T BREATHE!
SHE KILLED ONE OF THE QUEEN'S SACRED STYRS!
CURSE IT!
SHE DID SO TO SAVE ONE OF YOUR OWN. GIVE HER SOME AIR – AND HER FREEDOM!
HE'S RIGHT. GO AND GET SOME OF OUR SURFACE AIR ...
12A
SO, A LITTLE LATER ...
WE CANNOT KEEP YOU HERE. THE QUEEN WOULD TAKE REVENGE ON US!
OH? THERE'S A QUEEN!
YES – AS BEAUTIFUL AS SHE IS CRUEL. LEAVE THIS PLACE ... AND DON'T LISTEN TO THE ARCHANGEL'S BEWITCHING WORDS ...
THE ARCHANGEL?!
WE HAVE TO LEAVE, YOKO.
THE QUEEN WILL SOON TRACK THEM DOWN!
WHERE ARE YOU TAKING US, ARCHANGEL?
TO JOIN YOUR FRIEND, IF THAT'S STILL POSSIBLE.
12B

WHY DO THEY CALL YOU AN ARCHANGEL? ARE YOU A SUPERNATURAL CREATURE?

LET'S SAY I DWELL BETWEEN THE REAL AND THE UNREAL.

THE TRUTH IS THAT MY 19 COMPANIONS AND I MAKE UP A PRIVILEGED CASTE, SAFE FROM BIOLOGICAL CONCERNS AND THE RAVAGES OF TIME! IT HAS EARNED US SCORN FROM THE POWERFUL, AND HATRED FROM THE OPPRESSED ...

TWENTY ARCHANGELS! ... IMMORTAL?

IMMORTAL? NO! OUR LIFE WILL END WHEN THAT CITY DOES!

OH!

13A

AT THE BOTTOM OF A VAST HOLLOW, THE LOST CITY SPREADS BEFORE YOKO'S MARVELLING EYES ...

UP AHEAD ... THAT'S THE TOWER THAT SANK INTO THE WATER, ISN'T IT?

YES.

13B

THE TOWER IS HOW WE RENEW THE CITY'S ATMOSPHERE ...

... AND IT'S WHERE WE MUST GO WITHOUT BEING DETECTED ... BUT YOUR AIR SUPPLIES ARE INSUFFICIENT!

DO YOU HAVE A SOLUTION?

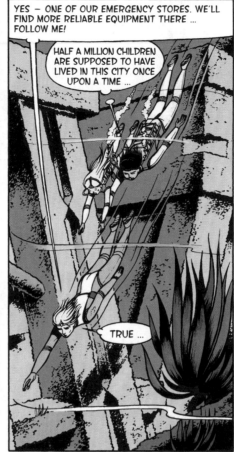

YES — ONE OF OUR EMERGENCY STORES. WE'LL FIND MORE RELIABLE EQUIPMENT THERE ... FOLLOW ME!

HALF A MILLION CHILDREN ARE SUPPOSED TO HAVE LIVED IN THIS CITY ONCE UPON A TIME ...

TRUE ...

... AND HALF OF THEM ARE STILL WAITING HERE FOR THE RIGHT TO BECOME ADULTS ...

HALF!! THAT'S A QUARTER OF A MILLION!

LOOK OUT!

14A

STOP BREATHING FOR NOW — WE DON'T WANT ANY BUBBLES!

WHAT IS IT?

MAINTENANCE ROBOTS! THEY'RE USED FOR OUTSIDE JOBS — BUT NEVER IN SUCH NUMBERS!

14B

THERE'S A WHOLE SQUADRON OF THEM! LOOKING FOR US? ...

NO.

THEY'RE HEADING TO THE RED PASS ... AND I HAVE AN IDEA WHAT THEIR OBJECTIVE IS!

OH? AND WHAT IS IT?

TO STEAL THE CHILDREN THAT WE RAISED AND EDUCATED!

ARE THEY GONNA HURT THEM?

NO, LITTLE POKY, BUT THEY WILL SWIFTLY DESTROY THE WISDOM WE PATIENTLY TAUGHT THEM!

OH! THE LIGHT'S COMING OUT OF HIS HEAD!

WE'RE HERE.

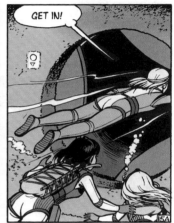

GET IN!

BECAUSE OF OUR CURRENT DEPTH, THE AIR PRESSURE IS HIGHER HERE.

YES – IT HURTS MY EARDRUMS!

IT WILL GET BETTER ... I'M INCREASING THE OXYGEN LEVEL SO YOU CAN BREATHE FREELY.

A LITTLE LATER ...

EXCELLENT! ASIDE FROM YOUR SKIN COLOUR, THE QUEEN HERSELF WOULD BE FOOLED. THE EXTRACTORS, NOW.

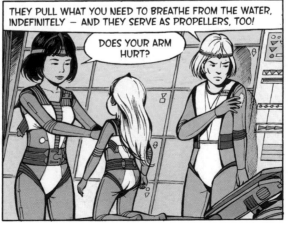

THEY PULL WHAT YOU NEED TO BREATHE FROM THE WATER, INDEFINITELY – AND THEY SERVE AS PROPELLERS, TOO!

DOES YOUR ARM HURT?

LET ME SEE! ARE YOU SCARED?!

SCARED THAT AFTER DISCOVERING MY TRUE NATURE YOU'LL NO LONGER TRUST ME ...

INTRIGUED, YOKO TOUCHES THE WOUNDED ARM ...

THAT'S FOAM ... WIRES ... **IS THIS A JOKE?!**

NO.

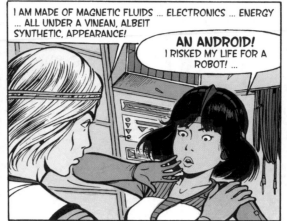

I AM MADE OF MAGNETIC FLUIDS ... ELECTRONICS ... ENERGY ... ALL UNDER A VINEAN, ALBEIT SYNTHETIC, APPEARANCE!

AN ANDROID! I RISKED MY LIFE FOR A ROBOT! ...

IF THOSE WHO CREATED US PERFECT AND SUPERIOR TO MAN COULD HEAR YOU ...

DID THEY ALSO IMBUE YOU WITH JOY, GRIEF ... AFFECTION, TENDERNESS, AND ... NO, I'LL STOP THERE!

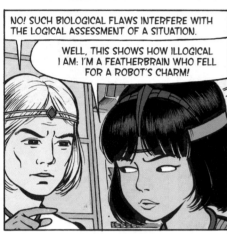

NO! SUCH BIOLOGICAL FLAWS INTERFERE WITH THE LOGICAL ASSESSMENT OF A SITUATION.

WELL, THIS SHOWS HOW ILLOGICAL I AM: I'M A FEATHERBRAIN WHO FELL FOR A ROBOT'S CHARM!

FOR NOW, THE ROBOT NEEDS YOU TO REPAIR ITS ARM.

FINE – THOUGH I'M NOT SURE I CAN ...

THE POWER CIRCUIT TO THE FLEXION PUMPS WAS SEVERED ... BYPASSING THE CUT BY PIGGYBACKING ON THE UNDAMAGED ROTATION CIRCUIT WOULD DO IT.

16A

HALF AN HOUR OF EFFORT LATER ...

WONDERFUL WORK! I ONCE AGAIN HAVE FULL USE OF MY HAND.

I MERELY FOLLOWED YOUR INSTRUCTIONS.

FORGET THE MACHINERY INSIDE ME AND BELIEVE ... IN MY 'FRIENDSHIP'!

I DO ... THAT'S MY WEAKNESS!

THE DEVICE IS HEAVY BECAUSE OF THE BALLAST REQUIRED FOR DEEPWATER USE ... ARE YOU BREATHING ALL RIGHT?

I AM.

I'LL EXPLAIN HOW TO CONTROL THIS OUTSIDE. JUST ONE LAST ADDITION AND WE CAN GO!

SOON, BACK OUTSIDE ...

YOU'RE DOING WELL!

THIS LITTLE AQUATIC SCOOTER IS A PLEASURE TO HANDLE!

16B

WITH YOKO FOLLOWING IN HIS WAKE, THE ANDROID WEAVES THROUGH THE BUILDINGS ...

IT'S A NETWORK OF MICROWAVE BEAMS THAT RETURN AN ECHO OF ANYTHING THAT CUTS THEM. WE'RE MAKING A DETOUR BY THE RED PASS ...

OH, SO THAT'S WHY WE'RE HEADING AWAY FROM THE CITY ... THE RED PASS. WHY THE NAME?

IF WE STAY ON THE BOTTOM, WE CAN AVOID THEIR DETECTION SYSTEM ...

HOW DOES IT WORK?

ITS CRESTS ARE COVERED IN REDDISH ALGAE ...

THAT'S THE DIRECTION THAT SQUADRON OF ROBOTS TOOK ...

EXACTLY! AND I BELIEVE THEY'RE NOT FAR FROM HERE.

LET'S STOP HERE. PUT THE SCOOTER DOWN ON THE FLOOR.

THE ROBOTS!! WHAT ARE THEY WAITING FOR?

WHAT'S COMING NOW FROM YOUR RIGHT.

I WAS RIGHT. LOOK, DOWN THERE!

OH!

INDEED, A BIZARRE MACHINE HAS JUST ENTERED THE GORGE ...

IT LOOKS LIKE A GIGANTIC CATERPILLAR!

THAT TRACTOR IS FULLY REMOTE-CONTROLLED. IN EACH OF THE CONTAINERS IT'S PULLING ARE ABOUT 50 SLEEPING CHILDREN. WE AREN'T EQUIPPED TO LET THEM GROW BEYOND THEIR TEENAGE YEARS.

OH? WHERE ARE YOU TAKING THEM, THEN?

TO A SAFE PLACE WHERE THEY WILL BE 'STORED', RESTING, UNTIL A SOLUTION CAN BE FOUND.

AN UNLIKELY PROSPECT FOR THESE AT THIS POINT!

OH! WHAT ARE THEY DOING?

ERASING THE AUTOPILOT'S MEMORY ...

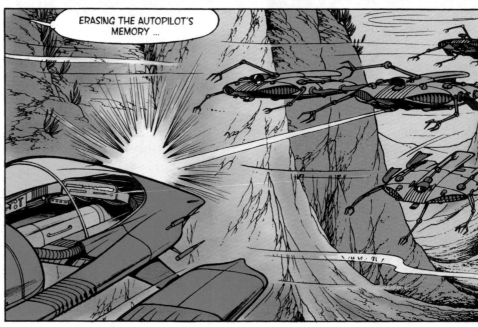

THERE! THE CONVOY IS IMMOBILISED ... ALL THEY HAVE TO DO NOW IS UNCOUPLE THE CONTAINERS AND LEAVE WITH THEIR PRECIOUS SPOILS ... AS THEY DO EVERY TIME ...

YOU LET THEM DO IT?

WE'RE NOT PROGRAMMED TO FIGHT THEM. THIS TIME, THOUGH, I HAVE WHAT WE NEED TO DEFEAT THEM! WILL YOU JOIN ME IN ATTEMPTING TO TAKE THE CHILDREN BACK?

GLADLY!

20

THESE SMALL DISCS ARE POWERFUL EXPLOSIVES. SINCE THEY'RE MAGNETIC, THEY'LL STICK TO METAL. JUST PULL THE RING TO ARM THEM!

UNDERSTOOD.

WE'LL USE THEM AGAINST THE ROBOTS THAT ARE BLOCKING THE WAY ... FOR THE OTHERS, YOUR DISINTEGRATOR WILL DO. AIM FOR THE MAGNETIC 'EYE' AT THEIR FRONT. POKY, ON MY BACK!

AND, SECONDS LATER ...

I'LL TAKE THE LEFT ONE, YOU TAKE THE RIGHT ONE!

ALL RIGHT — THOUGH THAT LEAVES THE MIDDLE ONE!

SLOWLY ... AND NOW THE CHARGE!

YOKO TAKES THE LIMPET MINE AND AFFIXES IT TO THE ROBOT'S BELLY ...

POK

ARM IT ... AND SCRAM!

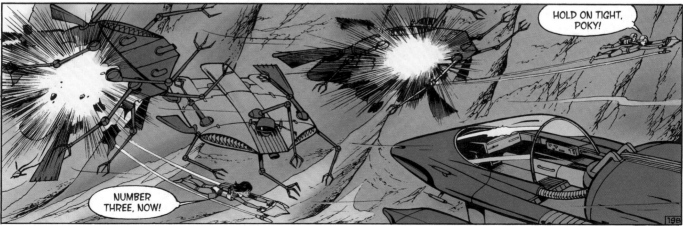

NUMBER THREE, NOW!

HOLD ON TIGHT, POKY!

THE THIRD ROBOT, HOWEVER, IMMEDIATELY GOES AFTER YOKO ...

DON'T STOP!!

FULL SPEED AHEAD ALONG THE CONTAINERS ... MY DISINTEGRATOR ...

... TO CLEAR THE WAY ... THE MAGNETIC EYE ... AND ...

AT THE LAST SECOND, AS YOKO DIVES UNDER THE BLINDED ROBOT, IT REARS UP STRAIGHT INTO THE PATH OF HER PURSUER ....

BINGO!

THE LAST ONE'S RUNNING!!

LEAVE IT! SEE IF THEY'VE UNCOUPLED THE LAST CONTAINER!

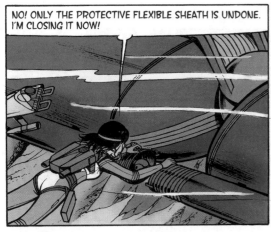

NO! ONLY THE PROTECTIVE FLEXIBLE SHEATH IS UNDONE. I'M CLOSING IT NOW!

AS SOON AS YOU'RE FINISHED, I'LL RESTART THE ENGINE.

ALL DONE — YOU CAN GO AHEAD ...

... I'M ON MY WAY ...

OH! THAT ROBOT'S BACK WITH REINFORCEMENTS!

WITHOUT A MOMENT'S PAUSE, YOKO GUNS THE ENGINE OF THE SCOOTER AND HEADS STRAIGHT FOR THE PACK ...

AIM RIGHT FOR THE MIDDLE ...

... ARM THE MINE ... BLOCK THE ACCELERATION ...

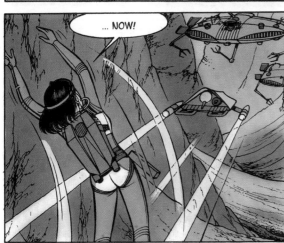

... NOW!

BUT, AS THE EXPLOSION SOWS CHAOS AMONG THE FORMATION, YOKO MAKES A TERRIFYING DISCOVERY ...

AHHHH!

MY PROPULSION UNIT'S NOT WORKING!

AND BEFORE THE IMMOBILISED YOKO HAS A CHANCE TO REACT ...

OWWW!

UNAWARE OF THE TRAGEDY TAKING PLACE BEHIND, THE ARCHANGEL HAS REDLINED THE TRACTOR'S ENGINES. BUT, AT THE END OF THE PASS ...

THEY'RE EVERYWHERE!

ONLY ONE WAY OUT: THE SURFACE! HOLD ON, POKY! WE'RE GOING UP.

I CAN'T SEE YOKO!

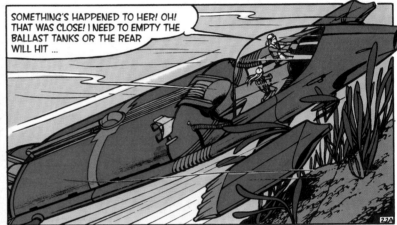

SOMETHING'S HAPPENED TO HER! OH! THAT WAS CLOSE! I NEED TO EMPTY THE BALLAST TANKS OR THE REAR WILL HIT ...

SUDDENLY LIGHTENED, THE MACHINE BOBS TO THE SURFACE LIKE A CORK ...

LOOK! A SHIP!

I SEE ONLY A MAN AND A CHILD AT THE CONTROLS OF THAT THING ...

THAT'S VYNKA! I CAN HEAR HIS VOICE!

24

NO DOUBT ABOUT IT. THAT'S POKY! ... BUT, WHERE ARE YOKO AND KHANY?!!

A LITTLE LATER ...

VYNKA!

POKY!

WE'RE ALL GOING BACK TO GET YOKO TOGETHER, RIGHT?

YES, POKY, BUT FIRST ASK THEM TO FOLLOW ME. I'M GOING TO BEACH THE CONVOY.

WHO IS THAT MAN? AND WHAT IS HE DOING?

HE'S AN ARCHANGEL ... HE'S CHECKING THAT THE CHILDREN ARE SLEEPING WELL ...

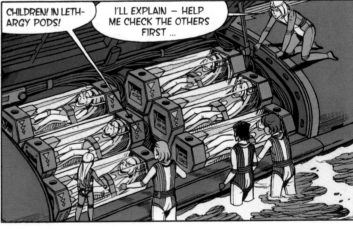

CHILDREN! IN LETHARGY PODS!

I'LL EXPLAIN — HELP ME CHECK THE OTHERS FIRST ...

AFTER A QUICK INSPECTION ...

NO DAMAGE! THAT'S GOOD. I CAN SAFELY LEAVE THEM WITH YOU.

CALL FOR REINFORCEMENTS. I'LL GO BACK TO RESCUE YOKO. I'D APPRECIATE THE TWO HUMANS' HELP, BUT I LACK ADEQUATE EQUIPMENT FOR THEM ...

THERE'S SOME IN THE SHUTTLE!

25

I THOUGHT THAT BLAST WAS GOING TO DISINTEGRATE ME ... BUT INSTEAD I'VE BEEN TURNED INTO A FIGUREHEAD! THIS IS HUMILIATING ...

OH! THERE'S THE QUEEN'S WELCOMING COMMITTEE.

RELEASE HER! AND YOU — AS LONG AS YOU DON'T TRY TO ESCAPE, NO HARM WILL COME TO YOU.

WHERE ARE YOU TAKING ME?

THE QUEEN WANTS TO SEE YOU.

THERE THEY ARE, YOUR HIGHNESS!

EXCELLENT! LET THE WATER IN.

SHE'S WAITING UP THERE.

IS IT PRUDENT TO EXPOSE YOURSELF SO, MY QUEEN?

ENOUGH! OPEN THE CUPOLA!

SO. THIS IS THE CREATURE WHO WREAKS HAVOC ON MY PLANS ...

... AND DESTROYS MY ROBOTS!

MERE MACHINES THAT YOU CAN REPLACE!

THE MACHINES, PERHAPS ... BUT WHAT ABOUT THE SACRED STYR?

I HAD TO KILL THAT ANIMAL TO SAVE A MAN!

SO YOU SAY. WILL ITS COMPANION, THOUGH? ...

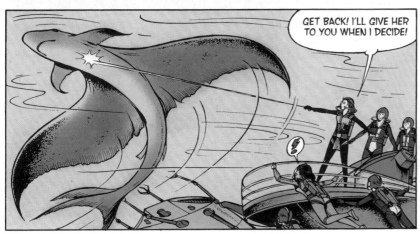

GET BACK! I'LL GIVE HER TO YOU WHEN I DECIDE!

EQUIP HER FOR COMBAT!

THE ROBOTS TOOK MY DISINTEGRATOR. I DON'T STAND A CHANCE!

A LITTLE LATER ...

FASTER!

TO TURN, OPEN THE TANK ON THE OPPOSING SIDE. TO GO STRAIGHT, OPEN BOTH. THEY WON'T LAST LONG ...

... BUT LONG ENOUGH TO BARREL ACROSS THE WHOLE ARENA AT FULL SPEED. THE QUEEN SENT HER GUARDS AWAY TO BETTER HEAR YOUR THOUGHTS AND GUIDE THE STYR ACCORDINGLY ... IT'S FAST BUT TURNS SLOW. MY BROTHER ONCE FIGURED IT OUT ... TOO LATE.

THANKS — I WON'T FORGET!

IF YOU TRY TO RUN, MY ROBOTS WILL CATCH YOU! IF YOU HOLD OUT UNTIL THE STYR TIRES OF THE GAME, THOUGH, I WILL SPARE YOU.

YOUR ROBOTS HAVE WARMER HEARTS THAN YOURS!

GO! SHE'S YOURS.

I MUST NOT THINK ... I MUST NOT THINK ...

JUST AS THE STYR IS ABOUT TO REACH HER ...

NOW!

AND NOW, THINK ... HARD!

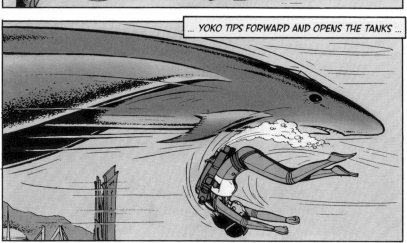

... YOKO TIPS FORWARD AND OPENS THE TANKS ...

28

ABANDONING HER SELF-IMPOSED MENTAL VOID, YOKO EVEN SPEAKS HER THOUGHTS OUT LOUD ... BUT CARRIES OUT THE OPPOSITE MANOEUVRE ...

IT'S TURNING LEFT ... I'LL CUT TO THE LEFT ...

SHE MADE IT TURN RIGHT!! I HAVE IT!!

THE ELECTRODES!

TANKS EMPTY! ... THE WIRES!

THE ANIMAL'S LEAPING AND TWISTING TO THROW YOKO OFF HAS BROUGHT IT BACK NEAR THE QUEEN ...

HOLD ON ... A BIT ... LONGER! ...

CURSE YOU! I'LL MAKE YOU LET GO!

... WHO POINTS HER ENERGY WHIP ... BUT THE STYR REARS UP SUDDENLY, AND THE BLAST AIMED AT YOKO HITS IT BEHIND THE EYE ...

GOT IT!!

BACK! NO! ...

AHHH ...

IMMEDIATELY, THE ROBOTS INTERVENE TO BRING THE STYR UNDER CONTROL ...

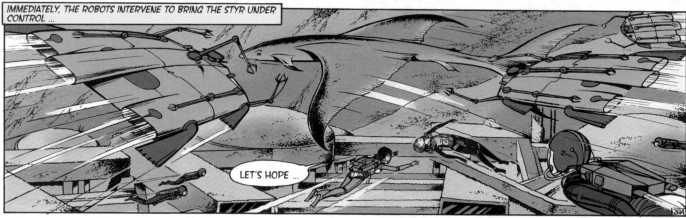

LET'S HOPE ...

MY LIFE IS DRAINING AWAY ... AND WITH IT THAT OF MY PEOPLE ... YOU'RE A CLEVER ONE, HUMAN. YOU WILL BE THE ONE TO ACCOMPANY ME TO THE CITY OF THE ABYSS ...

THE CITY OF THE ABYSS?!

HER!? SURELY NOT!? ...

YES, HER! ... SUCH IS MY WILL. BRING THE BATHYSCAPHE ... QUICKLY! ...

UH ... YES!

A LITTLE LATER ...

WHY ARE THEY ALL HANGING BACK LIKE THAT?

FEAR! EXPLAIN ... TO HER!

IT IS SAID THAT ON THE DAY QUEEN HEGORA PERISHES, SO, TOO, WILL THE CITY!

30

NOT FAR FROM THERE ...

THERE'S THE PALACE OF QUEEN HEGORA. OH! THAT'S A LOT OF ACTIVITY ABOVE THE ABYSS!

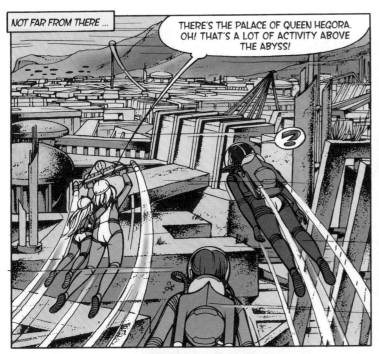

THESE TWO ARE ISOLATED ...

DON'T MOVE! ...

JUST ONE QUESTION: WHERE IS THE HUMAN?

WITH THE QUEEN ... THEY'RE TRAVELLING TO THE CITY OF THE ABYSS!

ALONE?

HEGORA IS HURT AND DEMANDED THAT THE EARTH WOMAN ACCOMPANY HER ON HER HEALING JOURNEY ...

NO ONE BUT THE QUEEN HAS EVER COME BACK FROM THE ABYSS!

WE HAVE TO GO AFTER THEM!

WE CAN'T – THE PRESSURE AT THAT DEPTH IS TOO GREAT. THERE'S ANOTHER WAY, THOUGH ...

SOON THE QUEEN'S BATHYSCAPHE REACHES THE BOTTOM OF THE CHASM ...

THE CITY! AT LAST!

YOU SEEM TO BE GETTING WEAKER, BUT I CAN'T FIND ANY VISIBLE INJURIES ...

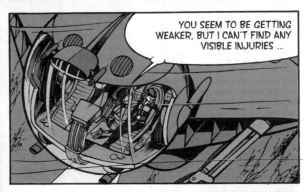

EVERYTHING IS ... DESTROYED ... INSIDE ME ... TAKE OFF ... BREATHING GEAR ... IN THE CITY ... SURFACE AIR ...

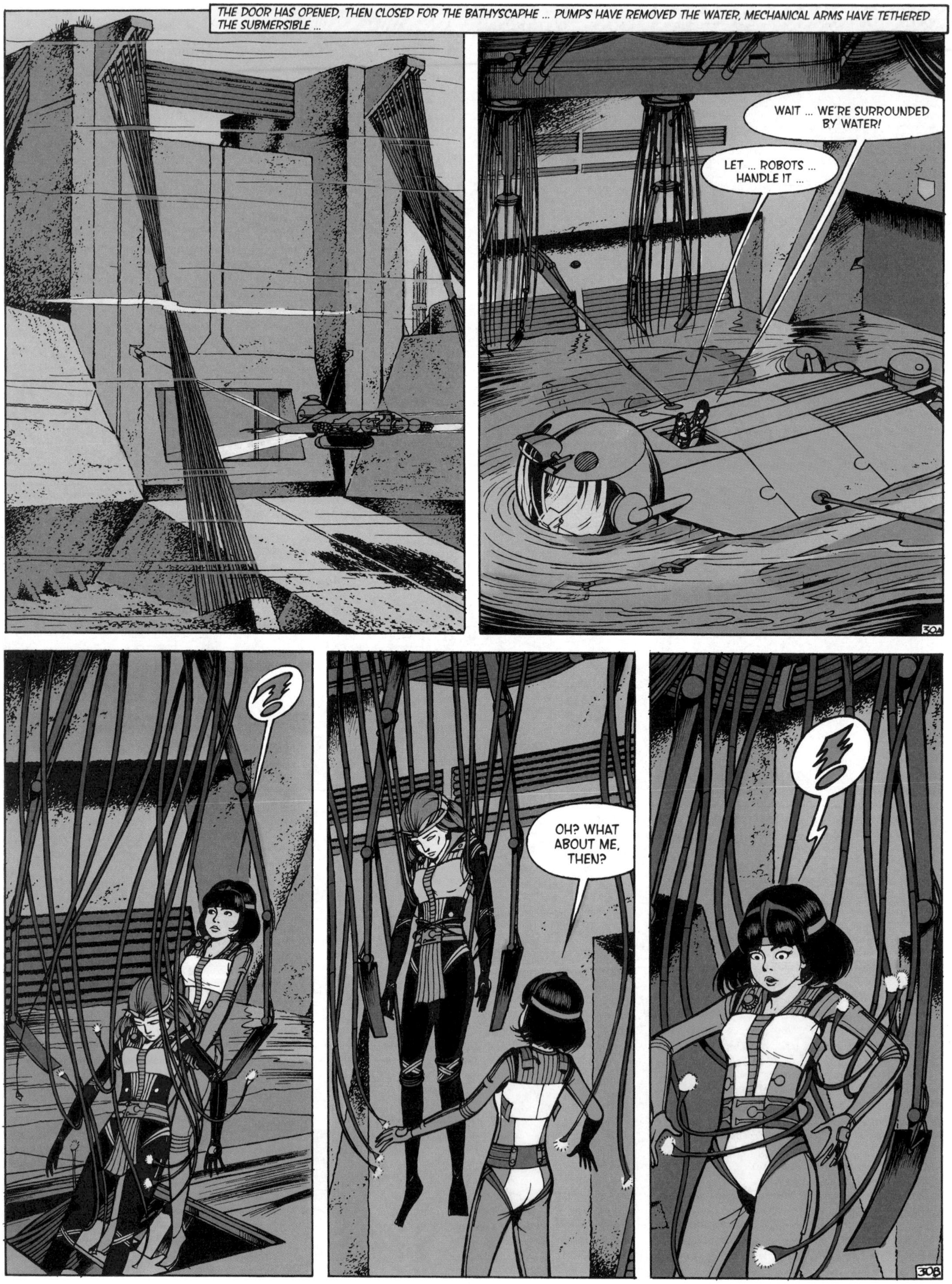
THE DOOR HAS OPENED, THEN CLOSED FOR THE BATHYSCAPHE ... PUMPS HAVE REMOVED THE WATER, MECHANICAL ARMS HAVE TETHERED THE SUBMERSIBLE ...
WAIT ... WE'RE SURROUNDED BY WATER!
LET ... ROBOTS ... HANDLE IT ...
30A
OH? WHAT ABOUT ME, THEN?
30B

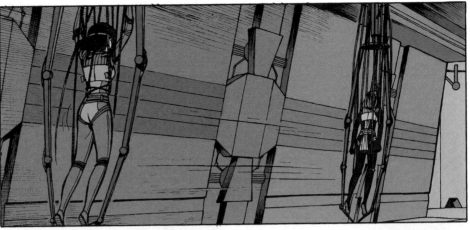

YOKO IS LIFTED BY THE ROBOT'S TENTACLES AND CARRIED BEHIND THE QUEEN ...

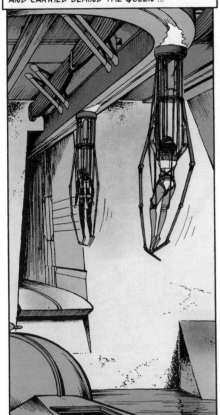

TO THE REGENERATOR ... HURRY!! ...

THAT ONE? WITH US. UNDER ... YOUR ... PROTECTION!

OW!

BOM

WHAT?! HEY!

WAIT FOR ME!

FOLLOW.

INCREDIBLE! ... THIS ROBOT'S VITAL PARTS ARE COMPLETELY UNPROTECTED!

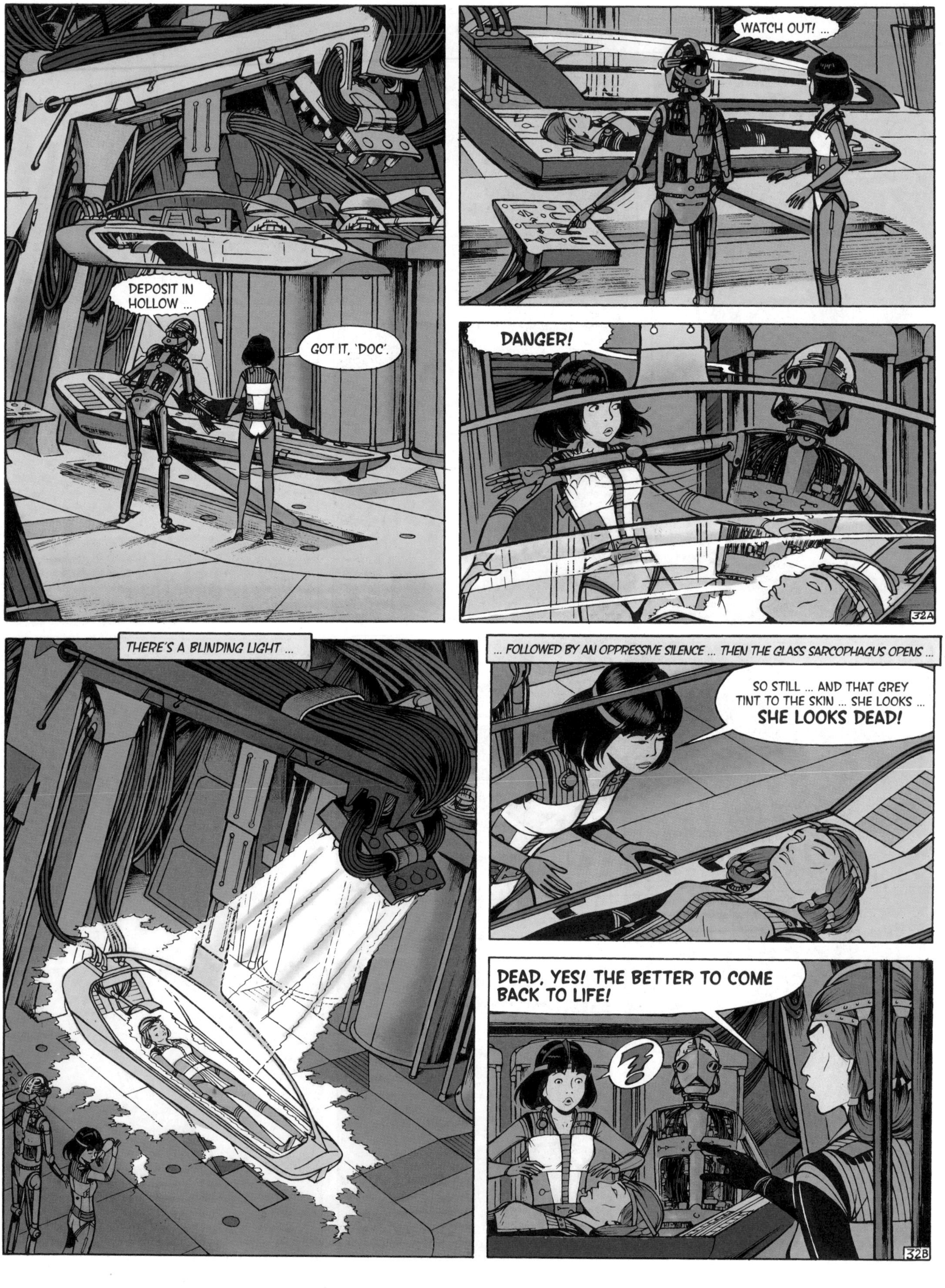
DEPOSIT IN HOLLOW ...
GOT IT, 'DOC'.
WATCH OUT! ...
DANGER!
32A
THERE'S A BLINDING LIGHT ...
... FOLLOWED BY AN OPPRESSIVE SILENCE ... THEN THE GLASS SARCOPHAGUS OPENS ...
SO STILL ... AND THAT GREY TINT TO THE SKIN ... SHE LOOKS ... SHE LOOKS DEAD!
DEAD, YES! THE BETTER TO COME BACK TO LIFE!
32B

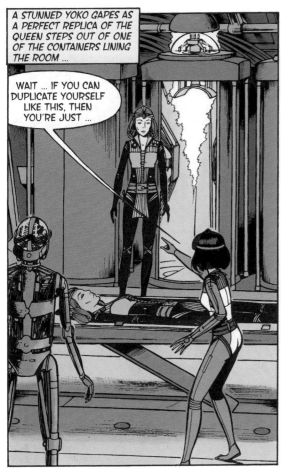

A STUNNED YOKO GAPES AS A PERFECT REPLICA OF THE QUEEN STEPS OUT OF ONE OF THE CONTAINERS LINING THE ROOM ...

WAIT ... IF YOU CAN DUPLICATE YOURSELF LIKE THIS, THEN YOU'RE JUST ...

YOKO RUSHES TO THE DEAD QUEEN, BUT THE ARM SHE GRABS CRUMBLES INTO DUST ...

WIRES, METAL ... AN AUTOMATON! A ROBOT!

SO, EACH ONE OF THOSE PODS CONTAINS ANOTHER IDENTICAL COPY OF YOU!

I HAVE FOUR LEFT. THAT LEAVES ME FIVE LIVES TO ACHIEVE MY GOALS!

FOLLOW ME! AS FOR YOU, GET RID OF THAT SAD PILE OF JUNK AND PREPARE FOR YOUR MENTAL REALIGNMENT.

Y ... YES.

REALIGNMENT ... ON WHAT?

ME, OF COURSE! NEW QUEEN, NEW PROGRAMMING ... IT'S OBVIOUS!

NO FLESH-AND-BLOOD BEING HAS EVER PASSED THIS FORBIDDEN DOOR!

SUCH AN HONOUR HAS TO BE SOME SORT OF TRICK!

ISN'T IT RATHER ABOUT ERASING ALL KNOWLEDGE OF YOUR PAST SELF FROM ITS MEMORY?

ENOUGH! IT'S NOTHING MORE THAN A CARETAKER ... NOW, COME!

GO. TRYAK WATCHES OVER YOU!

35

These rods go all the way to Vinea's magma, from which they extract energy ...

... And distribute it under the control of this super-computer. It's slaved to my brain and executes my every order ...

What's this noise?

TWEEP TWEEP TWEEP

A pulser that 'beats' to the rhythm of my electronic heart. Listen ... there, in my back.

What if ... your 'heart' were to stop? ...

TWEEP TWEEP

If my heart stops, the pulser stops ... IF I DIE, THE CITY DIES WITH ME!

It's ... diabolical!

I live, though, and my people will follow me anywhere ... Let's renew the air in the cities!

An entire people subjugated by a robot!

UP THERE, THE TOWER BEGINS TO RISE SLOWLY TOWARDS THE SURFACE ...

The tower's rising ... it's now or never!

36

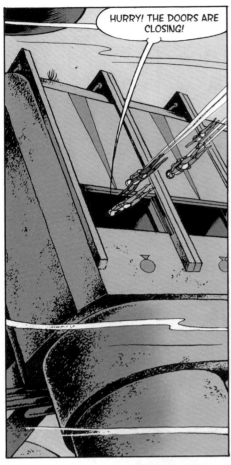

HURRY! THE DOORS ARE CLOSING!

THAT WAS CLOSE.

AND, AFTER A LONG DESCENT ...

WE'VE REACHED THE BOTTOM — HERE ARE THE PUMPS' FILTERS!

WE'RE GOING DOWN!

YES, TOWARDS THE CITY OF THE ABYSS ... AND AT THE TOP OF A WATER COLUMN, WITHOUT HAVING TO WORRY ABOUT INCREASING PRESSURE.

ONCE THE AIR IN HERE'S BEEN RENEWED, WE'LL LEAVE THROUGH THAT MAINTENANCE HATCH.

MEANWHILE ...

YOU WANTED TO SEE YOUR FRIEND? THERE SHE IS! ASLEEP, AND A PRISONER OF THE ARCHANGELS — WHO HAVE NO IDEA WHAT TO DO WITH HER, REALLY.

CLOSE UP ON THE ARCHANGELS ...

WHAT?! **THEY'RE IDENTICAL!!**

OF COURSE! WHICH IS WHY THEY HAVE NO PERSONALITIES ... NO NAMES! ...

THOSE ARCHANGELS ARE JUST THERE TO EDUCATE CHILDREN. LOOK!
LIKE A BATTERY FARM FOR CHICKENS. NO LOVE. IT'S INHUMAN!
THEY WOULD HAVE KNOWN GLORY ONE DAY IF THOSE FOOL ARCHANGELS HADN'T SPOILED EVERYTHING ... BUT, ONE DAY I WILL BEND THEM TO MY WILL ... AND VINEA WILL BE MINE! ...
... AS YOU ARE MINE NOW!
ME?!
UNNOTICED, YOKO HAS EDGED CLOSER TO THE QUEEN, AND ...
I DON'T BELONG TO ANYONE, AND YOU'RE GOING TO TAKE ME BACK UP!
STUPID GIRL! THIS WEAPON IS POWERED BY MY ENERGY ALONE! ...
... AND I HAVE BETTER WAYS TO SUBDUE YOU!
AHHHHH!
36A
I'M ONLY USING A TINY FRACTION OF MY POWER; OTHERWISE, YOUR FRAGILE LITTLE BRAIN WOULD DISINTEGRATE!
MY HEAD! NO! ... STOP! ...
CEASE! WHAT GOOD DOES TORMENTING HER DO YOU?
OH! SUCH HORRIBLE PAIN!
TRYAK! THE MORALISER! I'M GOING TO WIPE MORE THAN YOUR MEMORY THIS TIME!
!
JUST AS THE BEAM COMES OUT OF THE QUEEN'S FOREHEAD, THOUGH ...
AAAH! CURSE YOU! ...
36B

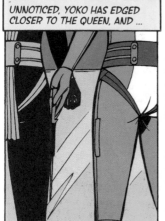

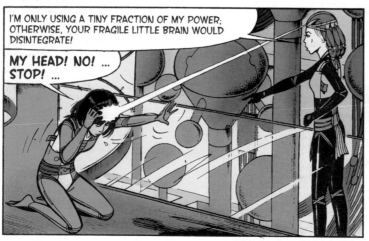

THEN I SHALL ERASE YOU FIRST!

AHHHH!

TRYAK! NO!

NO-O-O-O!!

THERE IS THE DULL SOUND OF THE BODY CRASHING FAR BELOW ... AND INSTANTLY, DARKNESS!

OH! I HOPE ...

BOM

WHY IS IT SO DARK?

THE QUEEN NO LONGER HAS MENTAL CONTROL OF THE CITY.

THE ELECTRONIC HEART BEATS ... BUT IT'S ALL OVER THE PLACE ... WE NEED TO TAKE HER TO THE REANIMATOR IMMEDIATELY!

ONCE SHE'S BROUGHT BACK TO LIFE, SHE'LL WANT TO KILL YOU AGAIN!

YOU MEAN ... **SHE'S DYING?!** WE MUST SAVE HER, TRYAK; OTHERWISE, **EVERYTHING WILL DIE WITH HER** ... WHY DID YOU DO IT?

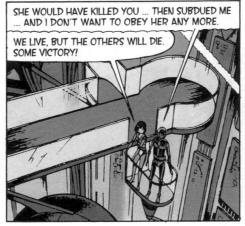

SHE WOULD HAVE KILLED YOU ... THEN SUBDUED ME ... AND I DON'T WANT TO OBEY HER ANY MORE.

WE LIVE, BUT THE OTHERS WILL DIE. SOME VICTORY!

A LITTLE LATER, THE QUEEN IS ONCE AGAIN INSIDE THE REGENERATION POD ...

THE COPY WILL IMPRINT ON THE FIRST CYLINDER. WATCH OUT — I'M OPENING IT NOW ...

IF THIS NEW QUEEN INHERITS THE PREVIOUS ONE'S INTENTIONS ...

... THEN IT WOULD BE WISE TO TAKE AWAY HER MEANS OF PERSUASION!

SWIFTLY, YOKO POPS THE RUBY OUT OF THE QUEEN'S DIADEM ...

POK

DONE, TRYAK!

SHE'S NOT MOVING. WHAT'S GOING ON?

NOT ENOUGH ENERGY. IT'S DISSIPATING!

BUT AS TRYAK REOPENS THE POD ...

IT'S INTACT ... THE TRANSFER DIDN'T TAKE PLACE! FORTUNATELY, THE HEART IS STILL BEATING.

TRYAK! THE COPY'S ALIVE!

IMPOSSIBLE!

FURIOUS, THE QUEEN'S COPY DISCOVERS THAT SHE NO LONGER CONTROLS THE SAME DESTRUCTIVE POWERS ...

THE ... THE CONCENTRATOR!

THE POD!

YOU TOOK AWAY MY WEAPONS BUT NOT MY STRENGTH! OPEN IT, OR I'LL PULL HER ARMS OUT!

OUCH!

YOU VILE CREATURE!

KLAK

40

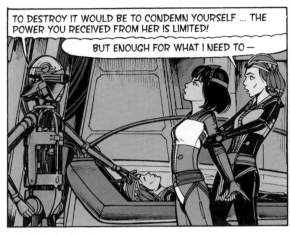

TO DESTROY IT WOULD BE TO CONDEMN YOURSELF ... THE POWER YOU RECEIVED FROM HER IS LIMITED!

BUT ENOUGH FOR WHAT I NEED TO —

YOU WILL DO NOTHING, HEGORA, EXCEPT SEE YOUR DESPOTIC REIGN END!

BY COMING IN HERE, ARCHANGEL, YOU HAVE BROKEN OUR PACT AND SIGNED YOUR PEOPLE'S DEATH WARRANT!

THE ARCHANGEL! VIC! POL!

LET ME PASS OR I'LL BREAK HER SHOULDERS! I SAID MOVE ASIDE!

GET BACK!

DON'T ... LISTEN TO ... HER! AHHHH ...

FOR HER SAKE, I ADVISE YOU NOT TO FOLLOW US!

JUST IGNORE ME! DO WHAT YOU HAVE —

WE DON'T EVEN KNOW WHERE SHE'S TAKING YOKO!!

I IMAGINE TRYAK MUST HAVE AN IDEA ...

KLAK

39A

SHE'S GOING TO TAKE ONE OF THE ARMED MODULES AND DESTROY THINGS UP THERE UNTIL SHE WINS!

EVERYTHING IS STILL SLAVED TO THIS ONE'S HEART, SO WE CAN DESTROY HER. WILL IT HOLD, THOUGH?

I CAN ASSIST IT INDEFINITELY!

GOOD! THEN, WARN THE UPPER CITY THAT AN IMPOSTOR IS COMING. VIC AND I WILL TAKE THE BATHYSCAPHE TO COUNTER HER.

MEANWHILE ...

MOVE!

ROCKETS?! WAIT ... THIS IS AN ARSENAL!

39B

41

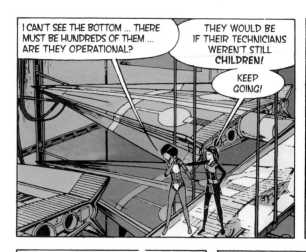

I CAN'T SEE THE BOTTOM ... THERE MUST BE HUNDREDS OF THEM ... ARE THEY OPERATIONAL?

THEY WOULD BE IF THEIR TECHNICIANS WEREN'T STILL CHILDREN!

KEEP GOING!

I GET IT NOW. IF NOT FOR THE ARCHANGELS' WISDOM, THE CHILDREN OF THIS CITY WOULD HAVE BECOME TECHNICIANS OF DEATH!

NO! OF REVENGE! OVER THE OTHER CITIES!

AHH! I STILL HAVE A USE FOR YOU!

REVENGE?! BUT ... THE CITIES YOU'RE TALKING ABOUT ARE ALL GONE! THEY DESTROYED EACH OTHER!

THEIR DESCENDANTS RULE OVER THE SURFACE OF VINEA ... WILL YOU MOVE?

ENOUGH! YOU'RE SLOWING ME DOWN!

PAK

OWW!

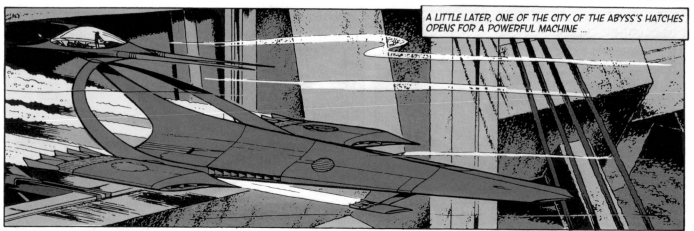

A LITTLE LATER, ONE OF THE CITY OF THE ABYSS'S HATCHES OPENS FOR A POWERFUL MACHINE ...

OH, MY HEAD! WHERE ARE YOU TAKING ME?

ON A PUNITIVE EXPEDITION. REMAIN NEUTRAL AND NOTHING MORE WILL HAPPEN TO YOU ...

... AS LONG AS ALL THE ARCHANGELS PLACE THE SAME VALUE ON YOUR LIFE!

TRYAK WAS RIGHT!

AFTER A QUICK ASCENT, THE QUEEN'S SHIP IS SKIMMING JUST ABOVE THE RUINS OF THE SUNKEN CITY ...

NO ONE! THEY'RE ALL HIDING IN TERROR! MY AUTHORITY IS INTACT.

AS FOR THOSE FOLLOWING ME, THEY'LL SOON BOW DOWN TO ME TOO!

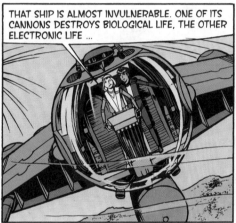

THAT SHIP IS ALMOST INVULNERABLE. ONE OF ITS CANNONS DESTROYS BIOLOGICAL LIFE, THE OTHER ELECTRONIC LIFE ...

YOKO CAN HELP US ... I KNOW HER MENTAL WAVELENGTH. I CAN COMMUNICATE A COURSE OF ACTION TO HER.

FINE, BUT NO UNNECESSARY RISKS!

OH, MY SHOULDERS! I HAVE NO STRENGTH IN MY ARMS ... WHAT? ... THE RED CASE? ... WHERE? ... OH, TO MY RIGHT ...

SO, THERE THEY ALL ARE! ... **WHAT?!** ...

UNDO THE SAFETY CATCH ... DONE!

INSTANTLY, THE RIGHT ENGINES STOP, AND, THROWN OFF-BALANCE, THE SHIP BANKS AND DIVES ...

AHHH!

... THEY'RE BLOCKING MY PATH! **TRAITORS! I'M GOING TO EXTERMINATE YOU!!**

DISCONNECT!

TSHAK

43

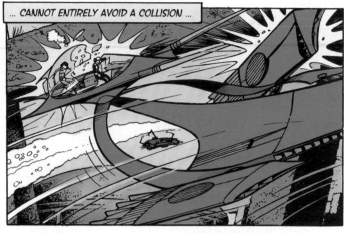

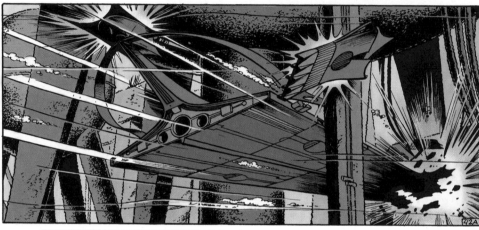

THE ROBOT WILL BE ON HER BEFORE WE ARE!

!

DELICATELY GRASPING YOKO, THE ROBOT QUICKLY MAKES FOR THE SURFACE ...

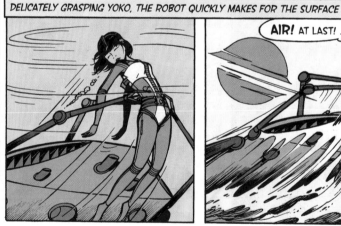

AIR! AT LAST! ...

A LITTLE LATER ...

I THOUGHT IT WAS GOING TO FINISH ME OFF; INSTEAD, IT SAVED ME ... THE QUEEN?

CRUSHED, ALONG WITH HER WARSHIP. AS FOR THE ROBOTS' CHANGE OF ALLEGIANCE, WE OWE IT TO TRYAK'S SKILLS OF PERSUASION!

THEN, GIVE US BACK KHANY AND LET US GO ... BECAUSE I'VE HAD IT UP TO HERE WITH WATER, ROBOTS AND ARCHAN ... SORRY. I'M CRACKING UP A BIT ...

I UNDERSTAND.

WE'RE GOING TO WAKE KHANY AND RETURN TO TRYAK ... HE HAS AN IMPORTANT REQUEST FOR YOU. I BEG YOU TO LISTEN TO HIM!

A REQUEST?

A FEW HOURS LATER, DOWN IN THE CITY OF THE ABYSS ...

I COULDN'T STOP HIM ...

... FROM GRABBING MY DISINTEGRATOR AND FIRING THREE SHOTS ...

WHY DID YOU DESTROY THE QUEENS, TRYAK?

BECAUSE ANY NEW COPY WOULD BE A MONSTER!

BUT, WHAT IF —

DON'T WORRY, YOKO. WE'LL TAKE THE FUTURE OF THESE PEOPLE IN HAND AND INTEGRATE THEM INTO OUR COMMUNITY.

AN UNREALISTIC SOLUTION!

OH? DO YOU SEE ANOTHER?

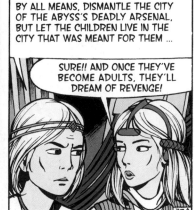

BY ALL MEANS, DISMANTLE THE CITY OF THE ABYSS'S DEADLY ARSENAL, BUT LET THE CHILDREN LIVE IN THE CITY THAT WAS MEANT FOR THEM ...

SURE!! AND ONCE THEY'VE BECOME ADULTS, THEY'LL DREAM OF REVENGE!

43A

THE SUREST WAY TO SPARK REVOLT AND A THIRST FOR FREEDOM IS ANNEXING THEM!

WHAT ABOUT YOU, TRYAK? YOUR OPINION? ...

AN AUTONOMOUS CITY ON VINEA? THAT'S DANGEROUS!!

THE CITY OF THE ABYSS MUST BE PLACED BACK UNDER MENTAL CONTROL; OTHERWISE, THE VINEANS' DESIRE FOR ORDER WILL MESS THINGS UP!

WHOSE MENTAL CONTROL?

MOMENTS LATER, IN A DIFFERENT ROOM ...

KHANY WILL NOT BE HAPPY! YOU'RE JEOPARDISING YOUR FRIENDSHIP!

I KNOW.

COME HERE.

WHY, YOURS, OF COURSE!! IF I ALIGN MYSELF MENTALLY TO YOU, EVERYTHING HERE WILL OBEY YOU ... THOUGH YOU'LL BE ABLE TO REJECT OR TRANSFER THAT POWER AT ANY TIME.

ME?!! TAKE HEGORA'S PLACE?! WHAT IF IT GOES TO MY HEAD? WHAT IF I START BEHAVING LIKE A QUEEN?

I TRUST YOU, AND THE PEOPLE UP THERE HAVE ACCEPTED YOU — OTHERWISE, THE ROBOT WOULDN'T HAVE SAVED YOU. COME ON. WE MUST ACT QUICKLY ...

WELL, WHY NOT, AFTER ALL?

43B

45

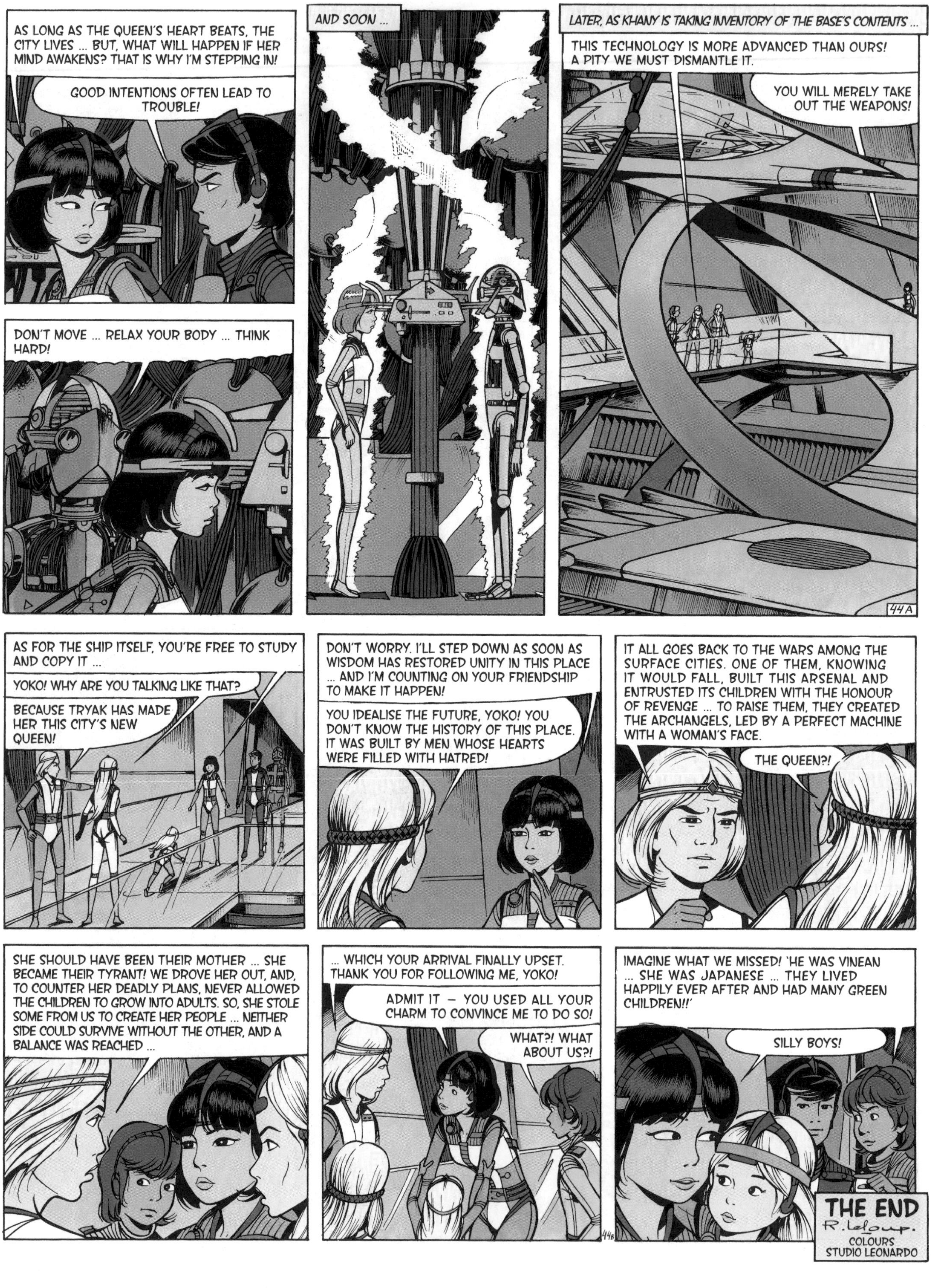
AS LONG AS THE QUEEN'S HEART BEATS, THE CITY LIVES ... BUT, WHAT WILL HAPPEN IF HER MIND AWAKENS? THAT IS WHY I'M STEPPING IN!
GOOD INTENTIONS OFTEN LEAD TO TROUBLE!
DON'T MOVE ... RELAX YOUR BODY ... THINK HARD!
AND SOON ...
LATER, AS KHANY IS TAKING INVENTORY OF THE BASE'S CONTENTS ...
THIS TECHNOLOGY IS MORE ADVANCED THAN OURS! A PITY WE MUST DISMANTLE IT.
YOU WILL MERELY TAKE OUT THE WEAPONS!
44A
AS FOR THE SHIP ITSELF, YOU'RE FREE TO STUDY AND COPY IT ...
YOKO! WHY ARE YOU TALKING LIKE THAT?
BECAUSE TRYAK HAS MADE HER THIS CITY'S NEW QUEEN!
DON'T WORRY. I'LL STEP DOWN AS SOON AS WISDOM HAS RESTORED UNITY IN THIS PLACE ... AND I'M COUNTING ON YOUR FRIENDSHIP TO MAKE IT HAPPEN!
YOU IDEALISE THE FUTURE, YOKO! YOU DON'T KNOW THE HISTORY OF THIS PLACE. IT WAS BUILT BY MEN WHOSE HEARTS WERE FILLED WITH HATRED!
IT ALL GOES BACK TO THE WARS AMONG THE SURFACE CITIES. ONE OF THEM, KNOWING IT WOULD FALL, BUILT THIS ARSENAL AND ENTRUSTED ITS CHILDREN WITH THE HONOUR OF REVENGE ... TO RAISE THEM, THEY CREATED THE ARCHANGELS, LED BY A PERFECT MACHINE WITH A WOMAN'S FACE.
THE QUEEN?!
SHE SHOULD HAVE BEEN THEIR MOTHER ... SHE BECAME THEIR TYRANT! WE DROVE HER OUT, AND, TO COUNTER HER DEADLY PLANS, NEVER ALLOWED THE CHILDREN TO GROW INTO ADULTS. SO, SHE STOLE SOME FROM US TO CREATE HER PEOPLE ... NEITHER SIDE COULD SURVIVE WITHOUT THE OTHER, AND A BALANCE WAS REACHED ...
... WHICH YOUR ARRIVAL FINALLY UPSET. THANK YOU FOR FOLLOWING ME, YOKO!
ADMIT IT – YOU USED ALL YOUR CHARM TO CONVINCE ME TO DO SO!
WHAT?! WHAT ABOUT US?!
IMAGINE WHAT WE MISSED! 'HE WAS VINEAN ... SHE WAS JAPANESE ... THEY LIVED HAPPILY EVER AFTER AND HAD MANY GREEN CHILDREN!!'
SILLY BOYS!
THE END
R. Leloup.
COLOURS STUDIO LEONARDO

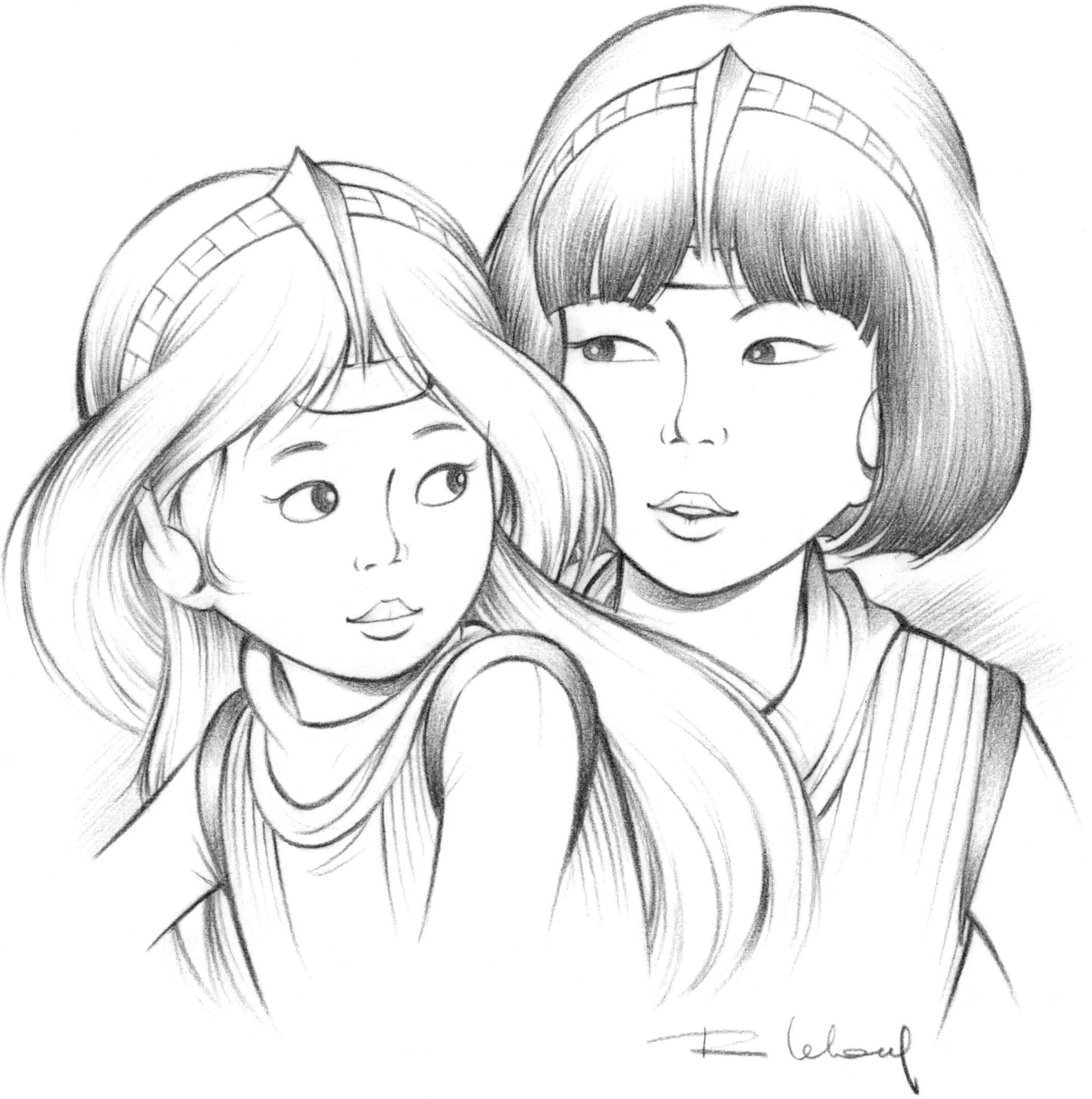

yoko tsuno
electronics engineer
by Roger Leloup

ON THE EDGE OF LIFE
THE TIME SPIRAL
THE PREY AND THE GHOST
DAUGHTER OF THE WIND

1 - ON THE EDGE OF LIFE

2 - THE TIME SPIRAL

3 - THE PREY AND THE GHOST

4 - DAUGHTER OF THE WIND

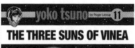

THE DRAGON OF HONG KONG
THE MORNING OF THE WORLD
THE CURIOUS TRIO
THE DEVIL'S ORGAN

5 - THE DRAGON OF HONG KONG

6 - THE MORNING OF THE WORLD

7 - THE CURIOUS TRIO

8 - THE DEVIL'S ORGAN

THE FORGE OF VULCAN
MESSAGE FOR ETERNITY
THE THREE SUNS OF VINEA
The Titans

9 - THE FORGE OF VULCAN

10 - MESSAGE FOR ETERNITY

11 - THE THREE SUNS OF VINEA

12 - THE TITANS

THE LIGHT OF IXO
THE ARCHANGELS OF VINEA

COMING SOON

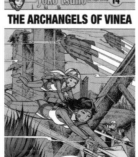

WOTAN'S FIRE

13 - THE LIGHT OF IXO

14 - THE

15 - WOTAN'S FIRE